HAMTARO'S NEW HOME

Adapted by Ruth Koeppel
Illustrated by Bill Alger

Scholastic Children's Books
Commonwealth House, 1-19 New Oxford Street, London WC1A 1NU
a division of Scholastic Ltd
London ~ New York ~ Toronto ~ Sydney ~ Auckland ~ Mexico City ~ New Delhi ~ Hong Kong

First published in the USA by Scholastic Inc., 2003
This edition first published in the UK by Scholastic Ltd, 2003

ISBN 0 439 96793 7

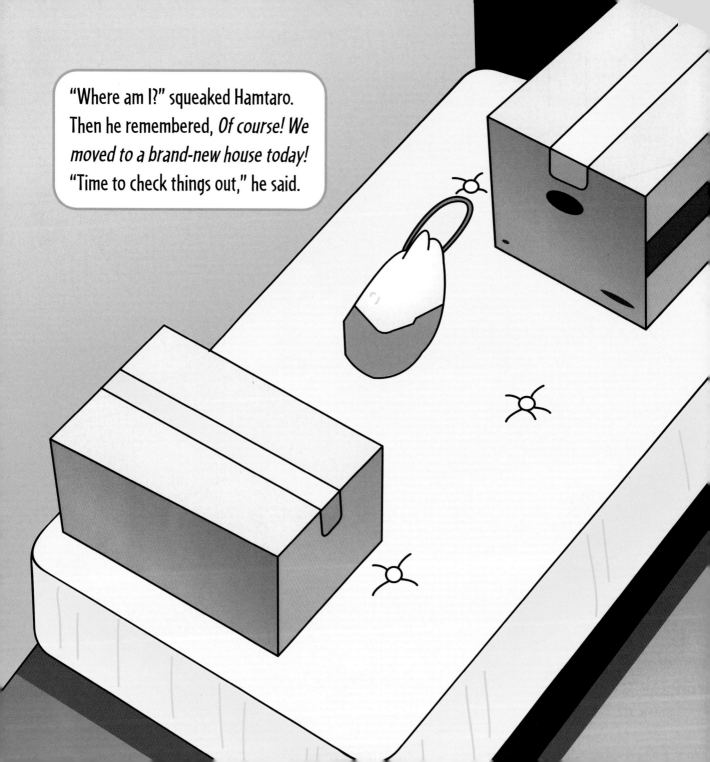

Hamtaro escaped from his cage and climbed up the curtains. "Hamtaro, you're chewing a hole in my new curtains!" cried Laura. She put him back into his cage. "Stay there while I finish unpacking."

After Laura left the house, Hamtaro looked out of the window. He couldn't resist a trip outside, so he slid down the drainpipe – and landed on Brandy's head! *PLONK!*

"Oops! Sorry, Brandy," Hamtaro said. "I didn't mean to wake you!"

Something was moving in the bushes. It was a big grey-and-white hamster.

"I've lost my sunflower seed!" cried the Ham-Ham.

"I'll help you look for it," said Hamtaro. "Two hamster heads are better than one!"

Hamtaro found the sunflower seed hidden behind a pebble.

"Thank you," said the other hamster happily. "My name is Oxnard."

Suddenly, Oxnard and Hamtaro fell down a hole into a big, dark cavern.
"Who is in *my* tunnel?" asked a scary voice.
Hamtaro and Oxnard huddled together in fear.
Was that the voice of a monster?

"You're not a monster!" said Hamtaro.

"No, I'm a wild field-ham," said a large brown-and-tan Ham-Ham.

"My name's Boss. And you've made a mess of my tunnel."

After Hamtaro and Oxnard helped to tidy up, Boss showed them round his underground home.

The three Ham-Hams climbed a tree outside Bijou's window.
Boss started to sing, but he stopped because he was too nervous.
Hamtaro and Oxnard joined in to help him.
Bijou tossed sunflower seeds to them!
"I think she likes you," Oxnard said to Boss.

Meanwhile, Laura was making new friends
too. While shopping, she met another girl
called Kana.
"I have a hamster named Hamtaro,"
said Laura.
"I have a hamster, too!" said Kana. "His name
is Oxnard. See you in school tomorrow!"

Hamtaro said goodbye to his new friends.

"See you soon!" he called out. Then he scooted back up his drainpipe.

Hamtaro slipped back into his cage just as Laura was arriving home.

"The hamster on my new notebook looks just like you, Hamtaro." she said.

"I'm going to keep a diary in it."

That night Laura wrote in her new diary. Hamtaro watched and ate sunflower seeds. *We just moved in today,* wrote Laura, *and already I'm starting to make new friends.* Hamtaro smiled between bites. He'd had an exciting day and was making new friends, too!

Laura picked up Hamtaro and he fell fast asleep in her hands.